A Note to Parents

Welcome to REAL KIDS READERS, a series of phonics-based books for children who are beginning to read. In the classroom, educators use phonics to teach children how to sound out unfamiliar words, providing a firm foundation for reading skills. At home, you can use REAL KIDS READERS to reinforce and build on that foundation, because the books follow the same basic phonic guidelines that children learn in school.

Of course the best way to help your child become a good reader is to make the experience fun—and REAL KIDS READERS do that, too. With their realistic story lines and lively characters, the books engage children's imaginations. With their clean design and sparkling photographs, they provide picture clues that help new readers decipher the text. The combination is sure to entertain young children and make them truly want to read.

REAL KIDS READERS have been developed at three distinct levels to make it easy for children to read at their own pace.

- LEVEL 1 is for children who are just beginning to read.
- LEVEL 2 is for children who can read with help.
- LEVEL 3 is for children who can read on their own.

A controlled vocabulary provides the framework at each level. Repetition, rhyme, and humor help increase word skills. Because children can understand the words and follow the stories, they quickly develop confidence. They go back to each book again and again, increasing their proficiency and sense of accomplishment, until they're ready to move on to the next level. The result is a rich and rewarding experience that will help them develop a lifelong love of reading.

For Andrea and Katelyn, with love
—C. S.

For my mother
—D. H.

Special thanks to Lands' End, Dodgeville, WI, for providing clothing.

Produced by DWAI / Seventeenth Street Productions, Inc.
Reading Specialist: Virginia Grant Clammer

Library of Congress Cataloging-in-Publication Data

Simon, Charnan.
    Wash day / by Charnan Simon ; photographs by Dorothy Handelman.
        p.   cm. — (Real kids readers. Level 1)
    Summary: While their father is napping, two boys enthusiastically wash everything in sight,
from dishes and toys to the rug and wall.
    ISBN 0-7613-2065-2 (lib. bdg.). — ISBN 0-7613-2090-3 (pbk.)
    [1. House cleaning—Fiction. 2. Cleanliness—Fiction. 3. Stories in rhyme.] I. Handelman,
Dorothy, ill. II. Title. III. Series.
PZ8.3.S5874Was   1999
[E]—dc21

                                                                    98-56272
                                                                    CIP
                                                                    AC

                        pbk: 10 9 8 7 6 5 4 3 2 1
                        lib: 10 9 8 7 6 5 4 3 2 1

Wash Day

By Charnan Simon
Photographs by Dorothy Handelman

M

The Millbrook Press
Brookfield, Connecticut

Dad wants to nap.
That is okay.

We will help him out
today.

I make big suds
in our new tub.

We get to work.
We rub and scrub.

A car? A jet?
A bat? A ball?

We dunk them in.
We wash them all.

I get a rag.

17

You get the mop.

We rub and scrub.
We do not stop.

We wash the rug.

We wash the wall.

We get stuff wet.
We wash it all.

We are wet too!
But we had fun.

29

We get Dad up.
Wash day is done.

31

Reading with Your Child

1. Try to read with your child at least twenty minutes each day, as part of your regular routine.
2. Keep your child's books in one convenient, cozy reading spot.
3. Read and familiarize yourself with the Phonic Guidelines below.
4. Ask your child to read *Wash Day* out loud. If he or she has difficulty with a word:
   - Help him or her decode the word phonetically. (Say, "Try to sound it out.")
   - Encourage him or her to use picture clues. (Say, "What does the picture show?")
   - Ask him or her to use context clues. (Say, "What would make sense?")
5. If your child still doesn't "get" the word, tell him or her what it is. Don't wait for frustration to build.
6. Praise your beginning reader. With your enthusiasm and encouragement, your child will go from one success to the next.

Phonic Guidelines

Use the following guidelines to help your child read the words in *Wash Day*.

Short Vowels
When two consonants surround a vowel, the sound of the vowel is usually short. This means you pronounce *a* as in apple, *e* as in egg, *i* as in igloo, *o* as in octopus, and *u* as in umbrella. Short-vowel words in this story include: *bat, big, but, Dad, fun, get, had, him, jet, mop, nap, not, rag, rub, rug, suds, tub, wet.*

Short-Vowel Words with Beginning Consonant Blends
When two different consonants begin a word, they usually blend to make a combined sound. Words in this story with beginning consonant blends include: *scrub, stop, stuff.*

Short-Vowel Words with Ending Consonant Blends
When two different consonants end a word, they usually blend to make a combined sound. Words in this story with ending consonant blends include: *dunk, help.*

R-Controlled Vowels
When a vowel is followed by the letter *r*, its sound is changed by the *r*. Words in this story with *r*-controlled vowels are: *are, car.*

Double Consonants
When two identical consonants appear side by side, one of them is silent. In this story, double consonants appear in the short-vowel words *will* and *stuff* and in the *all*-family words *all, ball, wall.*

Sight Words
Sight words are those words that a reader must learn to recognize immediately—by sight—instead of by sounding them out. They occur with high frequency in easy texts. Sight words not included in the above categories are: *a, and, day, do, I, in, is, it, make, new, out, that, them, to, too, up, wants, we, you.*